LUCI SOARS

Written and illustrated by Lulu Delacre

PHILOMEL

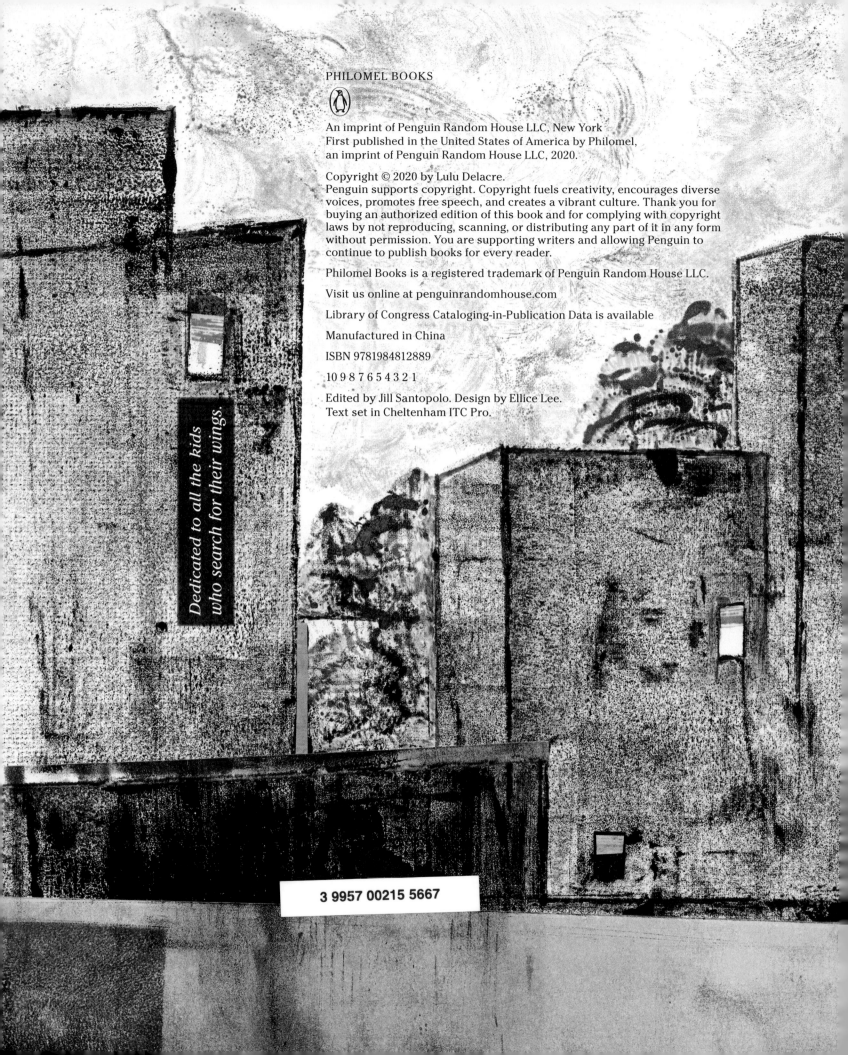

PHILOMEL BOOKS

An imprint of Penguin Random House LLC, New York
First published in the United States of America by Philomel,
an imprint of Penguin Random House LLC, 2020.

Philomel Books is a registered trademark of Penguin Random House LLC.

Visit us online at penguinrandomhouse.com

Library of Congress Cataloging-in-Publication Data is available

Manufactured in China

ISBN 9781984812889

10 9 8 7 6 5 4 3 2 1

Edited by Jill Santopolo. Design by Ellice Lee.
Text set in Cheltenham ITC Pro.

*Dedicated to all the kids
who search for their wings.*

I have no shadow.
Mamá says no one notices.
But I do.
And so do others.

In the beginning,
I didn't know I had no shadow.

"¡Qué linda!"
was the way
people saw me.
They didn't
know either.

But I grew up.

And people stared.

So I learned to walk
always in other people's shadows.

But I longed to be in the light . . .

. . . one day.

At school,
"one day" finally came.
I was brave.
One, two, three, four, five steps—

Mean shadows pointed.

Mean shadows laughed.

Mean shadows stared

their icy stares.

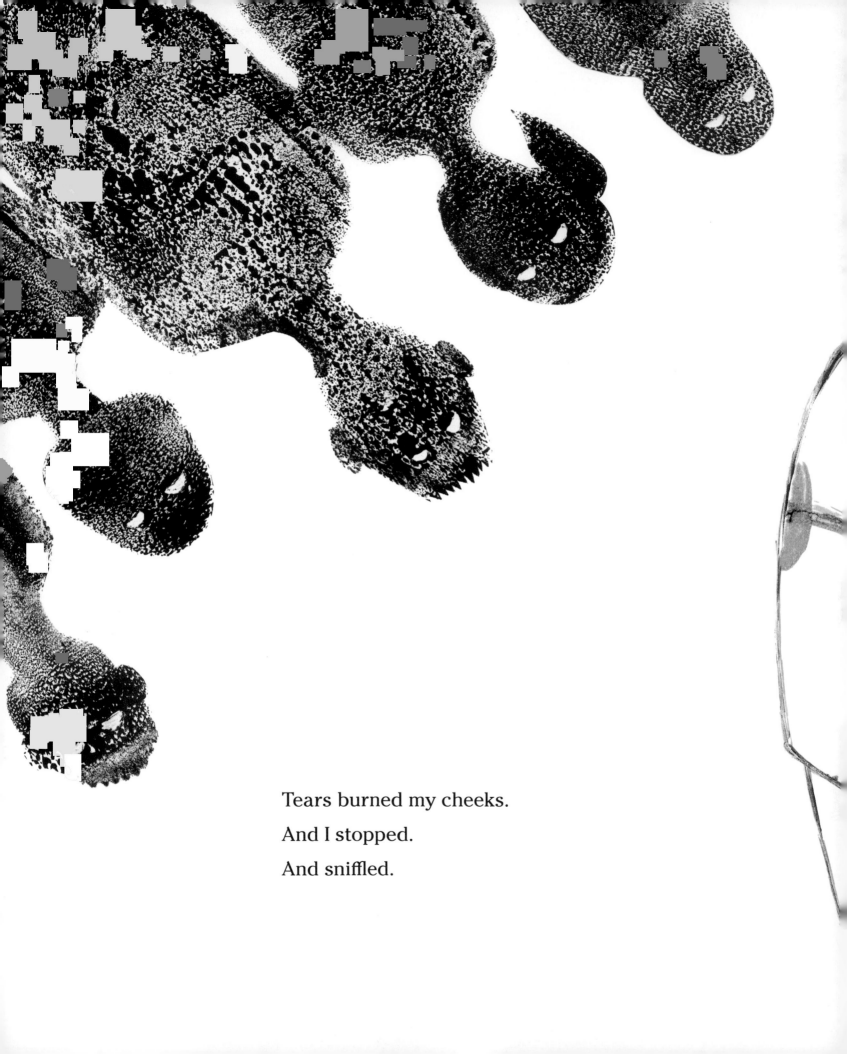

Tears burned my cheeks.

And I stopped.

And sniffled.

I wiped my eyes
and looked at the space

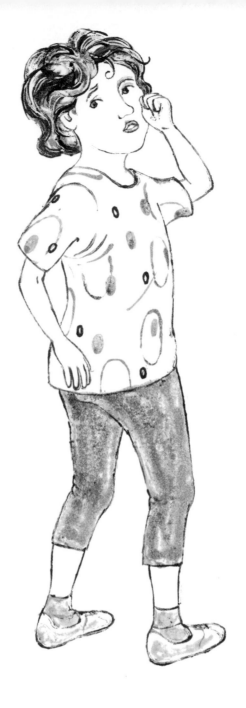

where I had no shadow of my own.

And I wondered . . .

Why do I need a shadow

anyway?

Does a shadow

keep you on the ground?

Something shifted
deep, deep inside me.

And outside, too.

"¡Mira!" I heard Mamá shout.

"¡Está volando!"

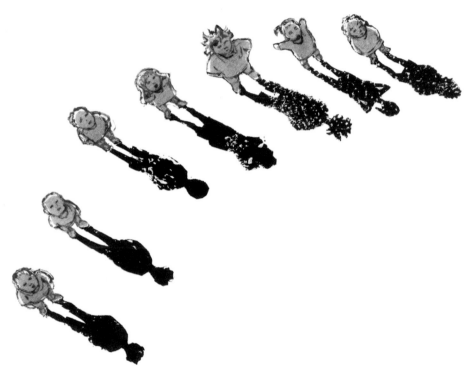

And the mean kids
with the shadows attached to the ground
gasped.

Silence.

I drifted.

The clouds tickled me
and made me smile.

Now I know
my superpower,
the superpower
that makes me strong.

I can change how I look at things . . .

. . . and so can you.